Night of the Full Moon

by Gloria Whelan

Illustrated by Leslie Bowman

Alfred A. Knopf 🐎 *New York*

THIS IS A BORZOI BOOK PUBLISHED BY ALFRED A. KNOPF, INC.

Text copyright © 1993 by Gloria Whelan
Illustrations copyright © 1993 by Leslie Bowman
All rights reserved under International and Pan-American
Copyright Conventions. Published in the United States of
America by Alfred A. Knopf, Inc., New York, and simulta-
neously in Canada by Random House of Canada Limited,
Toronto.
Distributed by Random House, Inc., New York.

Library of Congress Cataloging-in-Publication Data
Whelan, Gloria.
Night of the full moon / by Gloria Whelan ;
illustrated by Leslie Bowman.
p. cm.
Summary: When she sneaks away to visit her friend, a young
girl living on the Michigan frontier is caught up in the forced
evacuation of a group of Potawatomi Indians from their
tribal lands in the 1840s.
ISBN 0-679-84464-3 (trade)   ISBN 0-679-94464-8 (lib. bdg.)
1. Potawatomi Indians—Juvenile fiction. [1. Potawatomi
Indians—Fiction. 2. Indians of North America—Michigan—
Fiction. 3. Frontier and pioneer life—Michigan—Fiction.
4. Michigan—Fiction.] I. Bowman, Leslie W., ill. II. Title.
PZ7.W5718Ni 1993 [Fic]—dc20 93-6706

Manufactured in the United States of America
10 9 8 7 6 5 4 3 2 1

To Patricia Fagg

1

THE WINTER of 1840 was a snowy tunnel. We entered it in November and couldn't find our way out until April. Then spring surprised us. Almost overnight the white field by our cabin turned back into a pond. When Mama saw the last of the ice melt, she said to me, "Libby, it's like something heavy lifting from my heart."

Black-and-white bufflehead ducks sifted down onto our pond. The blue heron was back stalking frogs. One morning we heard the oriole sing and saw it flash through the

trees. Papa unraveled rope and hung the strands over branches. The oriole carried off the strands in its beak to weave into a nest that hung like a little bag at the top of an oak.

By June all the rows had pushed out green in our vegetable garden. I was kneeling pulling out weeds when Fawn appeared, like she always did—as softly and suddenly as a butterfly lighting on a flower. Her name was really Taw-cum-e-go-qua, but that was hard to say. Fawn was the name my papa made up for her. "She's like a young deer," he said. "Graceful, with those long legs and big eyes. Wary, too. I'm always afraid of startling her into skittering away."

Each fall Fawn and her family, along with the other Potawatomi Indians in their camp, went north to their winter trapping grounds. They didn't call themselves Potawatomi. They called themselves *Neshnabek,* which means "the People."

Fawn was splendid in a red and blue calico dress embroidered with red and blue beads. There was beading, too, on her deerskin moccasins. Her dark hair was braided with a red ribbon. "You have a new dress," I said. "And a ribbon." I'm afraid I was a little envious, for my own pinafore seemed dull, and I had no ribbons. Papa says beauty has nothing to do with fancy adornments, but I would have given anything to look like Fawn.

"The hunting was good this winter," Fawn said. "Each day in the forest the spirits of the animals called to my father. They told him where to put his snares and traps. He brought back many skins. At the store where he sold them he bought calico for me and my mother. I have another ribbon. I'll give it to you."

The Indians were always giving things away. When Papa was not able to find enough business as a surveyor to provide us with food for the winter, Fawn's papa brought us corn and wild honey and smoked fish. "Where did you make your winter camp?" I asked.

"We had to travel many nights' journey

from here to find the mink and the marten and the fisher."

It was true we had fewer animals, for as more and more settlers arrived, the woods where the animals once lived were turned into farms. Some settlers came as we did by covered wagon. Some came by boat through the new Erie Canal. A steamer called the *Governor Marcy* came all the way from Buffalo. It chugged down the Saginaw River, sending the ducks and geese flying. Soon the train would come to Saginaw. Everyone was buying up property. Now Papa had lots of land to survey.

"Did all the Indian families come back?" I asked Fawn. We had heard tales of smallpox in the north. The winter before it had spread like wildfire. Hundreds of Indians had died. Smallpox was a bad sickness for everyone, but because it was a white man's sickness it was much more serious for the Indians. So many Indians died of the disease they couldn't be buried properly and the wolves got at the graves.

"Two families from our clan did not return." For a long time Fawn was silent. When she spoke again it was in a voice so soft I could hardly hear her. "In the month of the longest nights my little brother, Namah, became sick. Sores covered his face and his body. He grew hot as though a fire burned inside him. He spoke in dreams. On the fifth day he died."

I remembered how Namah loved to trail after his father, Sanatuwa, and how his father had made him a small bow and arrows. I felt terrible.

The sadness stayed on Fawn's face. It only went away when she told me, "My mother has had a baby. It is a boy. He has a little red mark on the back of his neck just like my brother Namah had. Papa says Namah's soul has returned to us from *wojitchok,* the spirit land."

"We are going to have a baby, too," I told her. "Mama says it probably will be born in September. Papa says he'll make me a little room all for myself in the loft of our cabin so the baby's crying won't keep me awake at night."

Just then Mama came out to welcome Fawn. "How pretty you are," she said to her. "You look like a princess. I'm going to get my sketchbook and draw your picture." I hoped Fawn would let me try on her clothes someday. Then maybe Mama would draw a picture of me looking like a princess, too.

2

MOST DAYS Fawn worked in the cornfields or helped her mother sew and weave baskets. But whenever she could, she slipped away from the Indian camp to visit me. We went swimming in our pond, where the little minnows nibbled at our toes. We picked wild strawberries in June and wild raspberries in July. When Mama taught me my lessons, she taught Fawn too. Once Fawn brought a little deerskin pouch of colored beads and showed us how to embroider with them.

Fawn often came to see me, but I wasn't

allowed to visit her. The Indian camp was five miles away. Papa said it was too far for me to go by myself. It wasn't until the end of July, when two strangers knocked on our door, that I finally got to visit the camp.

The strangers said they were agents from the government. Papa invited them into our cabin. Mama gave them a drink of rhubarb juice. In the woods you were always hospitable to visitors. When there aren't many houses, you have to stretch friendship hard to make it go around.

One agent had hay-colored hair and a hat that was too big for him. He was shy about taking the rhubarb juice. He kept looking around to see if we were watching him drink it, which made us watch. The other agent had black eyes and black whiskers and didn't seem all that friendly. He drank his mug down all in one gulp. "Are there many Potawatomi Indians around here?" he wanted to know.

"Why do you ask?" Papa said.

"A lot of people think the Indians would

be better off away from the white men's settlements. There's wickedness goes on in towns that isn't good for the Indians to see. Better to have them far from all that. There's talk of sending them west across the Mississippi. They can have their own terri-

tory there. Someday there may even be an Indian state."

Papa said, "If you're talking of sending them someplace where men are always good and never sinful, I'm afraid you will have to wait for Heaven. When they talk of sending the Indians away, I think it is not the Indians' welfare that people have in mind. It is the taking of the Indians' land."

"What if the Indians don't wish to leave?" Mama asked. Her voice was angry.

The agent shrugged. "Topnebi has agreed to having his people sent west. Proper treaties have been signed by him giving Potawatomi land over to the government. After all, the Indians get paid for their land."

Papa said nothing, but I could see he was holding his tongue with difficulty. Once a year the Indians came to Saginaw from all over Michigan, hundreds and hundreds of them. They came to get their yearly payment. The government paid them because the Indians had sold land to the government. Papa would shake his head and say, "It is hard to see a people who once could ride for days and still be on their land now having to line up to get a few dollars from the government."

The agent caught the look on Papa's face. He said, "I must tell you the government means to enforce the treaties." When Papa didn't say anything, the agent stood up. "Well, we thank you for your hospitality. We were just passing through, but we may be back this way again."

I knew Papa was troubled, for as soon as the agents left he said, "I'm going to the Indian camp and warn them."

"Papa, let me come with you," I pleaded.

"Why not," Papa said. "You won't see a better day for a walk in the woods." He was trying to keep me from seeing how troubled he was, but I saw him exchange a worried look with Mama.

You learn more walking in the woods with Papa than you do in a dozen book lessons. We followed the trail the Indians made walking back and forth from their village to

camp. It was a small settlement with no more than five or six families. The families lived in wigwams. Fawn told me once that these are made from sheets of birch bark or mats of woven reeds laid over bent saplings. When the Indians moved to their northern hunting grounds, they just rolled up their reed mats and took them along. If we lived in a wigwam, I thought, Papa would be moving every week.

The Indians didn't pay us much attention, but all the village dogs ran out to sniff at us. They were skinny, which was just as well. Fat dogs got eaten. We found Fawn and her mother, Menisikwe. She welcomed us into their wigwam with the few words of English she had. A small fire burned inside. "To keep the mosquitoes away," Fawn said.

Their new baby was strapped to a board on Menisikwe's back. "You baby, too," Menisikwe said to Papa and me.

Fawn explained, "I told my mother about your baby. She is weaving a basket for the cradle."

"I hope our baby looks just like yours," I

said. Their baby had a perfect round face. His hair was glossy black like the wing of a crow. His eyes were like the black pebbles you see shining in a streambed.

While we admired the baby, Fawn ran to find Sanatuwa. Her father came to greet us dressed in a calico shirt and long buckskin leggings. A bright length of calico was wrapped around his head like a turban. In

his belt were a knife and a small axe. Like Fawn, Sanatuwa spoke English well. He and his family had lived near Detroit, where Sanatuwa had traded with white people. Fawn had gone to a missionary school there.

There were no chairs in the wigwam, only woven rush mats on the floor and on the wooden platforms that were used for beds. We all sat cross-legged on the floor while Papa told about the government agents.

Sanatuwa shook his head. "Some years ago the People south of here were rounded up. They were forced to leave their lands. They had to journey for many days to a place where nothing grew from the earth but stones. There was sickness. Many died on that trip. Now the white man has tangled one of our own chiefs in his web. That chief has signed away what little land we had left. All for money. Once we wanted only what we could make ourselves. Now we have learned to want things we must buy. But how can we leave our cornfields? How can we leave the holy places where our dead are buried?"

"I can't believe they will force you to go," Papa said. "But I thought it well to warn you."

"We thank you for telling us," Sanatuwa said. "But we must stay to harvest our corn. It may be when we go to our hunting ground this winter we will not come back."

My sadness must have shown on my face, for Sanatuwa said, "Let us hope it will not be so. Now we will talk of a happy thing. On the day of the next full moon we will have the naming ceremony for our new son. Our clan would like you and your wife and daughter to be our guests."

Papa said, "That would be a great honor."

Fawn and I exchanged excited looks.

On our way home Papa told me white men were seldom invited to such a ceremony. He smiled down at me. "With your skin so dark from the sun you could pass for an Indian yourself, Libby."

I began to daydream about how much fun it would be if I were Fawn's sister and could live with the Indians in their camp.

3

EVERY NIGHT from that night on I looked at the moon to try to guess how long before it would be full. It filled out so slowly I grew impatient. Then for three nights there were rain and clouds and I couldn't see the moon at all. At last Papa told me the next day would be the naming ceremony. Mama said Papa and I must go without her. "I'm as big as a barrel and the heat bothers me. It can't be many more days before the baby comes."

It wasn't. The next morning, just at bird-song, Papa shook me awake. "The baby is coming, Libby," he said. "I'm going to saddle up Ned and ride over to fetch Mrs. LaBelle. You must make your mother as comfortable as you can. Do just what she tells you." Before I could put my feet on the floor Papa was gone.

I was so scared I wanted to run after him. I made myself hurry to Mama. She was sitting up in bed, her hair still unbraided. Her lips were folded in tight, as if she was keeping something back. After a minute she gave me a skimpy smile. "Bring the baby's cradle, Libby, and the chest with all the things we've made." The cradle was the basket Menisikwe had made for us. Around the top she had sewn a braid of sweet grass so that the cradle was fragrant to smell. The baby would remember that pleasant scent all its life.

My hands were shaking as I took out the linen sheets I had helped hem and the shirts Mama had made that were so small she had let me try them on my doll. Mama told me what to do, but every couple of minutes she would have to stop and hold her breath and her lips would get tight again. I kept stealing glances out the window to see if Papa was coming.

Mama said, "Leave the things be, Libby. Tell me what you remember of our home in Virginia. I would give anything to be there today with our family and friends."

I sat on her bed and she held my hand. "Our house was painted white," I began. "There were four rooms, and my room had paper on the wall with leaves and little flowers."

"Ivy," Mama said, "and violets. How dainty they were." She looked at the plain, rugged log walls of our cabin.

"Your easel was in the sitting room, where you used to paint your pictures."

"Do you recall the garden?" Mama asked. Together we named the flowers: lilacs and bluebells and the Maiden's Blush roses. Every few minutes Mama would squeeze my hand so tightly it hurt.

Papa must have ridden hard, because it wasn't long before I heard the LaBelles' wagon coming up our trail. The LaBelles were the first family we had met when we came to Saginaw. When we put up our cabin, Mr. LaBelle had helped us.

Mrs. LaBelle, as tall and scrawny as a heron, marched in. She was all business, but you could see her gentleness in the way she put her hand on Mama's forehead. "Vinnie, don't you worry about a thing. I've seen to more births than I can remember. Rob, spread a blanket in front of the fire to warm. Libby, you're a good girl to have taken care of your mother. Now you must keep from getting underfoot. You can play outside until we call you."

"Papa," I said, "tonight will be the full moon. Today is the naming day for Fawn's little brother. Can't we go?"

"I couldn't leave your mother, Libby. You must see that."

I hung at the doorway. If I just looked disappointed enough I was sure Papa would change his mind.

Instead he became angry. "For shame, Libby! How can you think of your own self-ish pleasure at a time like this?"

Papa was right. I was cold-hearted. I should have been thinking of poor Mama. Only it seemed very hard to me to have to miss something I had looked forward to so much. Mama says I get my stubbornness from Papa. I was determined to go to the naming day. Fawn had told me there would be games and a feast. I said, "The wild blackberries on the other side of the pond are ripe." I added in what I hoped was a saintly voice, "I'll take the bucket and pick some for Mama."

"That's a good, thoughtful girl," Papa said. But I could tell that his mind was on following Mrs. LaBelle's commands.

As soon as I was outside I ran in the opposite direction of the pond. I headed for the pine woods and the trail that led to the Indian camp. Even though I had never gone to the camp by myself, Fawn had often come from there to visit me, and I didn't see why I shouldn't do the same. The path was a cushion of pine needles. Even my running made no noise. Soon I was out of the cool woods and in the meadow. Trees were scarce and the sun hot. When I came to a patch of wild blackberries, I hid the pail in a hollow tree. I would stop to pick some on my way back.

4

AT THE Indian camp there were all kinds of wonderful things to see. The Indians were gathered in the clearing in front of their wigwams. Some of the children were watching the Indian men dancing to the beat of a drum, while others were playing ball or wrestling. Everyone was dressed up. The men had painted their faces in stripes and patches of yellow and red and wrapped their heads in bright cloths. They looked like magical birds. The women wore necklaces and earbobs of silver and beads. Even the children's moccasins were embroidered with beaded flowers and leaves.

Fawn was looking for me. "Where are your mother and father?" she asked.

"Mama is having the baby," I said. Luckily Fawn did not question me more.

I hung back. Although everyone was friendly, suddenly I felt out of place. I tried to explain to Fawn. "Everybody looks so dressed up. I don't fit in."

Fawn smiled. "Come to our wigwam." She ran ahead of me. By the time I caught up with her, she had tumbled all the clothes from a large basket.

"Here is my other dress," she said. "Here are a pair of moccasins. And here is my ribbon I said you could have." Hastily I threw off my shift and slipped into Fawn's dress and moccasins. Fawn braided my hair with the ribbon and hung a necklace of beads around my neck. I longed to see myself in a mirror, but there was no mirror in the wigwam. We looked for Fawn's mama. Menisikwe was dressed in a bright calico shift embroidered with beads and fringed leggings sewn with ribbons. When she saw me, she threw up her hands. "No *chimokman*. You Indian today," she said, and laughed.

"What's a *chimokman*?" I asked Fawn.

"That's what we call people who are not Indians," she said. "Come, it is time for the food."

The women were putting out wooden bowls of cornmeal porridge swimming in maple syrup. There was fried fish and freshly roasted venison. There was some other meat. I hoped it was not dog.

The drums and dancing had stopped. "Where is your brother?" I asked Fawn.

"He is with my father and the other men from the clan." She pointed to where the men and young boys were gathered in a circle. "They are giving him his name. He is to be called Megisi. That means 'bald eagle.' It is a fine name because we are of the Eagle clan. The bald eagle is the largest of all eagles."

Suddenly, as though a great wind were blowing, the gathering of men and boys began to scatter. They ran first one way and then another. I thought it must be part of the ceremony until I heard Menisikwe and the other women cry out. Something in the woods was frightening them. Then I saw what it was. Mounted soldiers. They were riding into the camp.

They began to shout at the Indians. One of the soldiers shot his rifle into the air. Some of the Indians ran toward the woods, but the soldiers rode after them to bring them back. They were like the shepherd dogs in Virginia that ran barking and snarling at the sheep to herd them together.

I grabbed Fawn's hand. "What's happening?" I whispered, too frightened to speak aloud.

"It is what your father warned us of. They have come to take us away." Tears welled up in her eyes. That frightened me more than anything, for I had never seen Fawn cry. I began to cry, too. Desperately I looked around for Papa to help us. Then I realized how foolish I was. Papa was back home and didn't even know I was here.

One of the soldiers spoke Potawatomi. He shouted orders to the Indians. "What is he saying?" I whispered.

Fawn's voice trembled. "Our people will

be sent far away to live. They are taking us to join other clans of the People." Fawn caught her breath. "He says we must go at once to our wigwams to gather up whatever we wish to take with us. The men will be allowed to ride their ponies. They have brought a wagon for the women and children."

The sound of the women moaning and crying was terrible to hear. The men were shouting angry words at the soldiers. Fawn whispered, "Our men ask, 'What will happen to our cornfields and our sacred burial place?' "

Suddenly one of the Indian men ran at a soldier. I saw the flash of a knife in his hand. At once two soldiers were on him, wrestling him to the ground and tying him up.

Seeing the man bound by the soldiers, the other Indians seemed to lose heart. One by one the families turned slowly toward their wigwams. In Fawn's wigwam Menisikwe strapped Megisi to her back. She gathered up the baskets and the wooden bowls. She took her most precious possession, an iron kettle. Sanatuwa took his bow and arrows and his fishhooks. He took his flints and tinder so that he could make a fire.

We were about to leave the wigwam when Sanatuwa looked up. For the first time he noticed me. When he recognized me, he groaned.

The next moment he was pulling me after him toward the soldiers. When we reached a soldier on horseback, Sanatuwa called to him in English, "This girl is not of our clan. She is a white girl. She belongs to settlers who live near us. You must return her to her mother and father."

The soldier looked down at Sanatuwa. He seemed to be suspicious at finding an Indian who spoke English so well. He said, "If she's a white girl, why is she dressed in Indian clothes? What is she doing here with you?"

"I'm *not* an Indian," I insisted. I forgot how only an hour before I was longing to be one. "My name is Libby Mitchell." The soldier was not paying attention. He was watching two Indians who had rifles slung over their shoulders.

"Why won't you listen?" I cried, grabbing his reins. "I'm not an Indian! I don't want to be an Indian!" Suddenly I had an idea. "I'll show you the dress and shoes I came in."

"You probably stole them," the soldier said. He snatched the reins out of my hands and rode off to take the rifles from the Indians.

I turned to Sanatuwa. I was shaking. It wasn't just what was happening to me. It was what was happening to all of them: Fawn and her mother and father and all the members of her clan.

Sanatuwa shook his head. "I am sorry, but I can do no more now. I am the *okama,* the leader of my people. It is my duty to see to my clan, but I have not forgotten that when a sickness nearly took my daughter, your mother nursed her back to health. She saved my daughter's life. I will not let her lose her daughter." One of the Indians ran up to Sanatuwa to ask something. He nodded, taking a pouch from under his shirt. From the pouch he drew something strange. It looked like the dried head and neck of a bald eagle.

Fawn saw me staring at it. She whispered, "It is the sacred bundle, the *pitchkosan*, which holds the power of our clan."

A wagon rolled up to the camp. One by one the moaning women and weeping children climbed in with their baskets. Fawn and Menisikwe, carrying Megisi, got in. I thought, If I climb into that wagon I will never see Mama and Papa again.

I began to run toward the woods and the path that would take me home. A soldier came cantering after me. I could hear him calling, but I kept running. A moment later he swept me up onto his horse. The horse reared and he squashed me against him to keep me from falling.

I tried to tell him I was Libby Mitchell. "I don't care what your name is," he said. "An Indian is an Indian." I hit him with my fists. He only laughed at me. I was furious that he didn't believe me. I bit his hand, and he dropped me onto the ground. When he saw me start toward the woods again he pointed his rifle at me. "Get into the wagon!" he shouted.

I climbed into the wagon with the women and the other children, and the little procession pulled away, led by two soldiers. Next came the Indian men on their ponies and then our wagon. The rest of the soldiers followed. I looked over my shoulder.

Everything familiar was disappearing. I clung to the hope that by dinner Papa would miss me. But it was a long time till then. Besides, I had told him I would be in the opposite direction—across the pond. He would believe I got lost picking berries. He would never think of looking for me at the Indian camp. Even when he heard what happened to the Indians he would have no

reason to think I was with them. Soon I would be miles and miles away from Papa and Mama.

The wagon jogged along a trail so narrow that the tree branches scraped its sides. Ahead of us the Indian men were silent. They rode with closed, angry faces. I was praying we would go by way of Saginaw. I was sure I would see someone there who knew me and could tell the soldiers who I really was. But Fawn said, "We are going toward the sun, away from Saginaw."

We looked at each other, but neither of us said anything. When you are close to someone, words are slippery things that slide away from what you want to say. My hand stole into Fawn's hand as we sat there hanging on tightly to each other for comfort.

All afternoon the sun beat down on the wagon. It was hot and dusty. The wagon was so crowded that some of the children tried to climb over the sides, thinking to walk. The soldiers made them climb back in. The women were quiet now. Only the frightened way they clasped their baskets tightly to them showed what they were feeling. One of the soldiers, an older man with a long red beard, handed his water canteen to us. "Let the children drink from it," he said. His voice was gruff, but his eyes looked sad.

We were all tired and thirsty and relieved when the soldiers finally stopped and told us to make camp. The Indians had brought ground corn. Sanatuwa made a fire, getting sparks from his flint for the tinder, then fanning the tiny flame with a hawk's wing. The porridge was cooked in Menisikwe's iron kettle and shared out into wooden bowls, but we were too low-spirited to eat much.

There were about forty of us gathered around the fire. The men spoke in whispers. Even if I could have heard them, I wouldn't have understood what they were saying. Fawn explained, "It is a council."

Across the camping ground from us the soldiers were having their own dinner. They were talking loudly and laughing. Some of them were drinking out of bottles. Once or twice I thought again of trying to tell them who I was. But I was afraid, for there was a sentry on duty. Every time one of the Indians moved even a little way from our circle, the soldier pointed his rifle at him. The sentry kept watch long after we had wrapped ourselves in blankets and lain down.

I was ashamed to cry when the Indians could see me, but when I thought everyone was asleep, I couldn't hold back my tears. Fawn heard me. She whispered, "I know my father. He will not let a man tell him where he must go."

"What can he do?" I whispered back.

"He will find the right time," she said, and drew her blanket over her.

I lay there unable to sleep. Above us the full moon was so bright in the sky I couldn't see the stars that Papa used to name for me. I would have liked to have had them for comfort. At last I fell asleep. When I awoke the campfires had been lighted to cook our morning meal.

5

FOR TWO long, dreary days we traveled. On the third day we were told we would not stop until dark, that we were on our way to join up with another group of Potawatomi. Every mile we rode away from home stole more of my hope until there was little left. How could I have hope when all around me were the sad faces of the Indians? Like me, they were leaving behind everything they cared for. Only one thing kept me from despairing altogether. Sanatuwa had taken me aside and said, "I have not forgotten you.

Now my duty is to my clan. When we find a leader I can trust, I will give my clan's care over to him. Then I will return you to your people." I wanted to believe him, but I could not see how he would succeed.

It grew dark. When we thought we could travel no farther we saw ahead of us the light of campfires. They flickered like fireflies through the trees. We came upon a clearing with many Indians and soldiers. As we drew closer, the camp looked peaceful. The Indians and the soldiers were each gathered about their own campfires. But we knew the Indians were there against their will, for soldiers were patrolling the camp with their rifles at the ready.

As we climbed from the wagon several of the Indians ran up to us. Fawn said they were asking "What is your clan?" and "Where do you come from?"

Some of them had painted their faces black, a sign of mourning, Fawn said. She listened to their talk. "Members of the Otter clan are here, and members of the Wolf clan and the Turtle clan and the Bear clan. They were all taken, as we were, from their camping grounds. Like us, they will be sent far to the west. A great *okama* is here, too. They are saying that tonight he will speak for all of us."

Sanatuwa stood for some time, silently looking about him. At last he chose a place at the woods' edge. The Indians from the other clans gave us some of their food. As we were eating, a tall, elderly Indian man with feathers in his turban stood up in the middle of the camp and raised his arms for silence. Immediately everyone was quiet, even the soldiers. "He is a *kiktowenene*," Fawn said. "A speaker." The man spoke in English, for he was addressing the soldiers, but the Indians followed his words as closely as if he were speaking in Potawatomi.

"Hear me," he said to the soldiers. "Once we were brothers. Now you are using the trails made by our own people to carry us away from our camps. With your cunning you misled our chiefs. You tricked them into

signing away what was left of our fields and forests. Our children and the children of our children will never again see their land. Hear me. Even the wild creatures of the forest have a home, while our homes are taken from us. Hear me. We showed you how to hunt the deer and how to snare the beaver and the otter. What have you given us in return for what you have taken from us? You have given us sickness to destroy our bodies and whiskey to destroy our spirit."

The Indians murmured among themselves. Some of them began to beat drums. When one of the soldiers got up to put an end to the drumming, the soldier with the red beard motioned to him to let the drummers be.

The drumming went on far into the night. Tired as we were, it was hard to get to sleep. I was still awake when Sanatuwa tugged at my arm. He whispered, "The man who spoke tonight is a great *okama*. My people will be safe in his hands. My clan has not forgotten how your family nursed Taw-cum-e-go-qua when she was sick unto death. They agree that my duty is to return you to your family as your family returned my daughter to me. Tonight we will find our way from here. If we wait for another day we will be in country I do not know. You must seem to be asleep. Watch me and do what I do. When I move, you must follow me quickly. We must thank the Great Spirit for sending clouds to hide the moon tonight."

6

THE CAMPFIRES died down. We were in darkness except for the patrolling soldiers whose torches lit first one corner of the campground and then another. Fawn and I were wide awake, watching for Sanatuwa's signal. We waited so long I began to think that for this night he had given up the idea of an escape. In a way I was relieved, for I was afraid of what the soldiers would do if they caught us. Yet how I longed to see Mama and Papa. I must have drifted off to sleep because Fawn gave my arm a tug. "Hurry," she whispered. We inched our way toward Sanatuwa and Menisikwe, who were already halfway into the woods. Menisikwe was carrying Megisi on her back.

Luckily the ground under us was damp, so the leaves did not rustle. When we were free of the clearing, Sanatuwa motioned us to follow him. A moment later, like moths in candle flame, we were caught in the glare of a rush torch. It was one of the sol-

diers, the soldier with the red beard. I saw Sanatuwa's hand move toward the small axe he carried in his belt. Then a surprising thing happened. The soldier, instead of reaching for his rifle, said, "Why should you not walk as freely as I do?" He turned his back and headed toward the camp.

"Quickly," Sanatuwa whispered. He seemed to know the path even in the dark.

I could see nothing. I tripped over a log and fell. Then I took a wrong turn and bumped into a tree. Fawn took my hand and pulled me along with her.

It felt as though we had been running for hours when Menisikwe called something to Sanatuwa and he stopped. "We will rest here," he said. "I forget Libby is not used to our traveling." While we rested Menisikwe nursed Megisi. Watching them, I thought of my own brother or sister nestled in my mama's arms, and tears slid down my cheeks.

At first I was too afraid to fall asleep, but my eyes soon closed. I was awakened by the sound of a woodpecker hammering on a nearby tree. It was such a friendly sound I thought I was at home in our cabin. I waited to hear Mama's soft voice coaxing me out of bed. Instead I heard Sanatuwa say, "Come, we must find a better place before the sun is up. This morning when they discover we are gone they will send soldiers to look for us. If we get away, they know others will surely try."

We left the path and made our way to the banks of a small stream. Gratefully we drank the cold water. It sparkled like jewels in the sun as it fell from our hands. Menisikwe mixed the water with cornmeal she had brought with her. We could not risk a fire to boil the porridge. I was so hungry I didn't care that it tasted like grainy paste. With the gentle sound of the water and the grassy banks of the stream fragrant with mint, I was sorry to leave. It seemed such a safe place.

I thought we would try to cover as much ground as possible. Instead Sanatuwa led us away from the stream and into a sparse wood that was a tangle of tall grass and briers. With a stab of remorse I saw that the briers were wild blackberry. I thought of all the trouble I had caused by my stubborn willfulness and my lie about picking blackberries. "Fawn," I said, "if it weren't for me, your papa and mama wouldn't have run away from the soldiers. They wouldn't be in all this danger."

Sanatuwa overheard me. "You are right

to say that I led us away from the soldiers because it was my duty to return you to your father. It is true that otherwise I might have remained in the camp. But there is no need to hang your head for being the means of our freedom."

I wasn't sure, but I thought what Sanatuwa said was that he was glad they had run away. That made me feel better. Menisikwe, who had gone on ahead, had disappeared. Now she called to us. We couldn't see her, but her voice sounded close by. Suddenly she stood up. She was only a few feet from us. She had hunched down in a place where the tall grass had been flattened into a wide circle. "Deer bed," she said.

"We will stay here," said Sanatuwa. "If we travel through the woods, the soldiers will overtake us with their horses. But they will spend no more than one day looking for us. If they don't find us today, they will give up."

As we hunched down into the nest of grass, we could look up at the tops of the trees swaying in the wind. A white-throated sparrow was singing. Yellow swallowtail butterflies hung from the clusters of goldenrod. Fawn asked if she and I could go over to the wild blackberry bushes to pick some berries. Sanatuwa said we might and Menisikwe gave us a basket.

We filled the basket and stuffed ourselves as well. We knew we had to be quiet, but it was hard not to laugh at how our mouths and hands were stained red from the juicy berries. The berries were delicious. The sun felt warm on our backs. We nearly forgot why we were there until the sound of horses sent us running. We dived into the circle. Two soldiers galloped by so close we could smell the sweat from their horses. Megisi began to whimper. Hastily Menisikwe put her hand over his mouth. In a moment the soldiers were gone. I was too frightened to say a word, but Sanatuwa said, "They have finished looking here. They will not come this way again." He smiled with satisfaction.

As soon as it was dark we started off again. At first we traveled through the woods, keeping away from the trail. After a while Sanatuwa led us back to the trail, and the way became easier. We never rested for more than a moment or two. Early the next morning we slept for a few hours hidden among tall ferns in a little copse of trees. By afternoon I told Fawn that I was sure I could not go another step.

"Do you not know where we are?" Fawn asked. She was smiling. I looked around. We were in the pine forest, on the path that led to our cabin. A moment before, my feet had been too heavy to lift. Now I ran faster than I had ever run in my life.

7

"WHERE HAVE you been? Oh, Libby, where have you been?" Mama cried. She threw her arms around me. "Your papa is out with a posse of men looking for you. We searched everywhere. Were you lost in the woods? How did you find your way back? Why in heaven's name are you dressed like an Indian?"

Mama was squeezing me so tightly I could hardly get out the words "Sanatuwa and Menisikwe and Fawn brought me back."

For the first time Mama noticed them

standing silently at the door. Leaving me for a moment, she drew them into the cabin. "Thank goodness you are safe! We had heard that all the Potawatomi had been taken west by the soldiers." Mama looked more puzzled than ever. "But how did you find Libby?" Her arms were back around me, and I could feel her tears against my cheek. "I thought we would never see you again."

We told Mama the story. When Papa came back, we told it all over again. Then Mama and Papa wanted to hear it another time. All the while Mama was getting food for us. She coaxed Menisikwe and Sanatuwa and Fawn and me to eat more and exclaimed over Megisi. "We can't ever thank you enough," Mama said to Sanatuwa. "You risked your lives to bring Libby back to us."

"What will you do now?" Papa asked. "The soldiers may come back. You and your family must stay with us. They won't think of looking for you here."

"We will stay for a day and a night," said Sanatuwa. Fawn and I smiled at each other. We would be together for another whole night and a day. "Then we will go to the north, to our winter hunting grounds at L'arbre Croche. Some of the People live there all year around with the Ojibwa. We will be welcome and we will see no soldiers that far north." Hearing that her family might leave forever, Fawn and I were no longer smiling.

Just then we heard loud crying. Menisikwe hurried across the room. "Ahhh," she said. She was looking into the cradle she had woven. In all the excitement I had forgotten about the baby.

"Like Fawn, you have a little brother, Libby," Papa said. "Better get acquainted with William."

I ran to look at the new baby. He was so small. I reached down to take my brother's hand. His tiny fingers curled around my finger.

Sanatuwa stood beside me. "That is a fine boy," he said.

Mama said, "Menisikwe, you had better teach me to carry William on my back as you do Megisi. We too may be traveling north. No sooner do we have a comfortable cabin and neighbors close by than my husband talks of moving." Mama didn't sound very happy.

"So far it is only a dream," Papa said. "But

things are changing here. I have been hired to survey land for a canal from Lake Huron to Lake Michigan. Think of the people that would bring! In our village of Saginaw plans have been drawn up for a town with four hundred blocks. That is not a town; it is a city! We are sorry to see you and your family leave us, Sanatuwa, but we may be neighbors again one day."

I wasn't sure I wanted to leave our cabin for a place in the north woods. But I wasn't sure, either, if I wanted to say good-bye forever to Fawn.

Fawn and I whispered far into the night. "Will you promise always to be my friend? No matter how far away you go?" I asked Fawn.

"Always," she promised. "It will be as if you are one of our clan." She took the small silver eagle on a string of rawhide from around her neck and gave it to me. I gave her my bracelet with the tiny gold heart that had belonged to my grandmother.

In the morning Papa had a plan.

"Sanatuwa, it is the law that if an Indian buys his land he is not subject to treaties. He cannot be sent away."

"But I own no land," Sanatuwa said. "And I have no money to buy land."

"I have land," Papa said. "More than I need. I will give you some. It is a small return for risking your lives to bring Libby back to us. That way you would not have to leave."

Sanatuwa was quiet. Fawn and I held our breath. At last he said to Papa, "You are a good man, but I cannot take your land. I would own the land, but the land would also own me. I would be like a dog chained to a post."

Papa sadly shook his head. "I will not try to persuade you against your will, Sanatuwa, for I feel too much as you do."

Mama filled a basket with food. Papa gave Sanatuwa a rifle so he could hunt on the way north. Then we watched our friends walk down our path, past the pond, and into the woods.

Author's Note

Although *Night of the Full Moon* is fiction, the story is based, in part, on various accounts of the removal of the Potawatomi Indians from Indiana and southern Michigan in 1840. Throughout the summer of that year, soldiers of the U.S. Army, under Brigadier General Hugh Brady, rounded up the Potawatomi from their homes and villages. On August 17, over 500 Potawatomis embarked on a forced migration to Kansas, leaving their homelands behind forever.

Gloria Whelan

is a poet and short-story writer who has also written many books for children, including *Next Spring an Oriole, Silver, The Secret Keeper, Hannah,* and *Goodbye, Vietnam.* She lives with her husband in the woods of northern Michigan.

Leslie Bowman

was born in New York City, grew up in Connecticut, and graduated from the Rhode Island School of Design. She recently began a fruitful career as an illustrator of children's books; her published works include *Snow Company, The Canada Geese Quilt,* an ALA Notable Book, and *Hannah,* also by Gloria Whelan. Leslie Bowman lives in Minnesota.